Farmer George
and the Hedgehogs

Other titles featuring
Farmer George are:

*Farmer George
and the Fieldmice*

*Farmer George
and the Hungry Guests*

*Farmer George
and the Lost Chick*

*Farmer George
and the New Piglet*

*Farmer George
and the Snowstorm*

Farmer George
and the Hedgehogs

Nick Ward

PAVILION

For Fern and Charlie.
About time too!

First published in Great Britain in 1999 by
PAVILION BOOKS LIMITED
London House, Great Eastern Wharf
Parkgate Road, London SW11 4NQ

This edition published 2001

Text and illustrations © Nick Ward

Designed by Ness Wood at Zoom Design

A CIP catalogue record for this book is available
from the British Library.

ISBN 1 86205 526 2

Set in Bell MT
Printed and bound in Singapore by Kyodo
Colour origination in Hong Kong by AGP Repro (HK) Ltd.

2 4 6 8 10 9 7 5 3 1

This book can be ordered direct from the publisher. Please contact
the Marketing Department. But try your bookshop first.

Late one autumn morning, Farmer
George was in his cottage garden,
raking up the fallen leaves.
"Ooh my back aches," he complained.
"And it's cold!"

"Don't carry on so!" smiled Dotty,
the farmer's wife, handing him a mug of
hot chocolate. "It's a lovely morning."

The cold air made Dotty's rosy cheeks
tingle. "I'm going to do some baking,"
she said.

Farmer George worked through the
morning, raking leaves into his
wheelbarrow and emptying them onto
a large pile of garden rubbish.
"I think I'll have a bonfire and get rid
of this mess," he said.

Dotty was in the kitchen, rolling and kneading dough to make some bread. Glancing out of the window, she saw a wisp of smoke curling over the cottage garden wall.

"What is that silly billy up to,
Tam?" she asked the dog.
"I've told him bonfires can
be dangerous."
"Very dangerous!" barked Tam.

Dotty was marching across the yard to tell Farmer George off, when she saw a little hedgehog scampering along in front of her. His spines were covered in bits of twig and leaves.

"He must be toddling back to his nest to hibernate for winter," chuckled Dotty.

And then a terrible thought crossed her mind. "Oh no!" she cried, and grabbing a bucket of water she raced to the cottage garden.

"Marvellous," said Farmer George as little flames started to take hold of the leaves.

But just then Dotty hurtled into the garden and threw the bucket of water over the fire.

The bonfire went out and Farmer George got soaked.

"What on earth's the matter?" he gasped. "I was only burning rubbish!"

"Fires are dangerous," said Dotty. "Look!" and she lifted up the top layer of twigs.

There underneath, three damp and sleepy hedgehogs blinked their eyes in the autumn sunshine. "Is it spring already?" they grumbled.

"Oh dear," said Farmer George.
"I didn't know. What are we going to do with them?"

"Well they can't stay here," said Dotty.
"It's much too damp now. We'll have to find them somewhere else to hibernate.
But where?"

Farmer George and Dotty took all four hedgehogs to the hen house.

"Too noisy!" grunted the hedgehogs.

Next they tried
the stable.

"Too dangerous," they cried, seeing
Sidney's huge, stamping hooves.

"What about the pigsty?" asked
Farmer George.

"Too muddy," said Dotty.
"And too smelly!" squealed the
hedgehogs.

"Well where can they stay?" asked the farmer. Dotty had a think and looking down at Tam, she said, "I think I know the perfect place."

"Not my basket!"
yelped Tam.
"Don't make such a
fuss," smiled Dotty.
"They'll be safe and
warm here."

And she wrapped Tam's blanket
around the hedgehogs and placed a
saucer of bread and milk nearby.

"But where am **I** going to sleep?"
barked Tam.
"Don't worry," laughed Farmer George,
seeing Tam's worried expression...

"You'll have to sleep on our bed!"

So for the whole of that winter, Tam snuggled down at the foot of the farmer's bed, and the hedgehogs snored through the frosty days and freezing nights, all cosy and dry in Tam's basket.

Ssh... don't wake them!

Oh dear! The wind has blown away the pile of leaves. Can you count how many Farmer George will have to collect?